WELCOME TO
PASSPORT TO READING
A beginning reader's ticket to a brand-new world!

Every book in this program is designed to build read-along and read-alone skills, level by level, through engaging and enriching stories. As the reader turns each page, he or she will become more confident with new vocabulary, sight words, and comprehension.

These PASSPORT TO READING levels will help you choose the perfect book for every reader.

 READING TOGETHER
Read short words in simple sentence structures together to begin a reader's journey.

 READING OUT LOUD
Encourage developing readers to sound out words in more complex stories with simple vocabulary.

 READING INDEPENDENTLY
Newly independent readers gain confidence reading more complex sentences with higher word counts.

 READY TO READ MORE
Readers prepare for chapter books with fewer illustrations and longer paragraphs.

This book features sight words from the educator-supported Dolch Sight Words List. This encourages the reader to recognize commonly used vocabulary words, increasing reading speed and fluency.

For more information, please visit passporttoreading books.com

Enjoy the journey!

D1044305

Little, Brown and Company
Hachette Book Group
1290 Avenue of the Americas, New York, NY 10104
Visit us at LBYR.com
mylittlepony.com

First Edition: October 2019

Little, Brown and Company is a division of Hachette Book Group, Inc. The Little, Brown name and logo are trademarks of Hachette Book Group, Inc.

The publisher is not responsible for websites
(or their content) that are not owned by the publisher.

Library of Congress Control Number 2019944551

ISBNs: 978-0-316-49040-5 (pbk.), 978-0-316-49039-9 (ebook), 978-0-316-49043-6 (ebook), 978-0-316-49038-2 (ebook)

Printed in the United States of America

CW

10 9 8 7 6 5 4 3 2 1

Passport to Reading titles are leveled by independent reviewers applying the standards developed by Irene Fountas and Gay Su Pinnell in *Matching Books to Readers: Using Leveled Books in Guided Reading*, Heinemann, 1999.

Licensed By:

We Are Thankful

by R. R. Busse

LITTLE, BROWN AND COMPANY
New York   Boston

**Attention, My Little Pony fans!
Look for these words when you read this
book. Can you spot them all?**

sanctuary

castle

club

sibling

My name is
Princess Twilight Sparkle.
I live in Equestria
with all my friends!

My friends and I often think about everything we are thankful for.

I am thankful for Pinkie Pie.
Pinkie throws parties
and bakes yummy treats.

She makes us laugh!

Rarity loves fashion
and makes outfits
for everypony
in Ponyville.

I am thankful that she is so
generous with her talent.

I am thankful Applejack
is an honest friend.

She is always ready to
help anypony in need!

Fluttershy treats each
animal in Equestria
with kindness.

She even has an animal sanctuary!
Our furry friends are
thankful for her care.

Rainbow Dash is loyal and fast.

We are thankful that she helped
us earn our cutie marks!

Spike is my best friend!

He is messy,

but he is brave!

I am thankful for my home,
the Castle of Friendship!

It is the perfect place to keep
my books, and it is next
to my School of Friendship!

Anycreature who wants
to learn about friendship
is welcome at my school.

The students are all
thankful to be there.

Sweetie Belle, Scootaloo, and
Apple Bloom go to a different school.

Everypony is thankful that their
club, the Cutie Mark Crusaders,
helps other ponies find
their cutie marks.

We are all thankful to live
in a town like Ponyville.
Everypony looks out
for one another here.

I live in Ponyville because
of Princess Celestia.
I am thankful she is
such a great teacher.

She teaches me all about
the Magic of Friendship!

Princess Luna is Celestia's sister.
They had a big fight, but
they are good friends now.

Luna and Celestia are
thankful for each other.

I have a sibling, too!

His name is Shining Armor.

He is married to Princess Cadance,
and they have a baby named
Flurry Heart.

I am thankful for the advice and
love my family gives me.

We are thankful for the
new friends we make!
They are from around
Equestria and are
all so different!

24

Their differences make
each of them special.

Starlight Glimmer is a new friend.
She was not always nice.

Now Starlight Glimmer is
learning about friendship.

She lives in the
Castle of Friendship, too!
I am thankful she is
my student.

Trixie is another new friend.
She used to play tricks on ponies,
but she does not anymore.

Starlight Glimmer is thankful
Trixie is her friend!

Fluttershy is thankful for Discord.
He used to try to confuse
ponies with his magic.

But now he is our friend
and helps on our adventures!

We are thankful for the
Magic of Friendship most of all!

With the Magic of Friendship,
we can do anything!

What are YOU thankful for?